D1500291

CHLOE *by* DESIGN

FASHION WEEK
Finale

BY MARGARET GUREVICH

ILLUSTRATIONS & PHOTOS BY BROOKE HAGEL

STONE ARCH BOOKS
a capstone imprint

Chloe by Design is published by Stone Arch Books
A Capstone Imprint
1710 Roe Crest Drive
North Mankato, MN 56003
www.capstonepub.com

Library of Congress Cataloging-in-Publication Data
Gurevich, Margaret, author.
Fashion week finale / by Margaret Gurevich; illustrations by Brooke Hagel.
pages cm. -- (Chloe by design)

Summary: Fashion Week passes in a whirlwind of activity, and when it is over
Chloe's summer internship is at an end, but before she packs up and heads
back to California and high school, she gets a gift from the designers she has
worked with — and a surprise invitation.

ISBN 978-1-4965-0507-1 (hardcover) -- ISBN 978-1-4965-2313-6 (ebook pdf)

1. Fashion design--Study and teaching (Internship)--Juvenile fiction.
2. Fashion designers--Juvenile fiction. 3. Internship programs--Juvenile
fiction. 4. Friendship--Juvenile fiction. 5. New York (N.Y.)--Juvenile fiction.
[1. Fashion design--Fiction. 2. Internship programs--Fiction. 3. Friendship--
Fiction. 4. New York (N.Y.)--Fiction.] I. Hagel, Brooke, illustrator. II. Title. III.
Series: Gurevich, Margaret. Chloe by design.
PZ7.G98146Fas 2016
813.6--dc23
[Fic]

2014043696

Designer: Alison Thiele
Editor: Alison Deering

Artistic Elements: Shutterstock

FEB 2 3 2017

Printed in the United States of America in Stevens Point, Wisconsin.
042015   008824WZF15

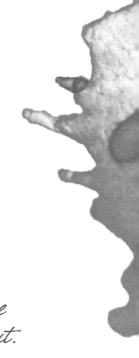

Measure twice, cut once
or you won't make the cut.

Dear Diary,

Where has the time gone? I can't believe I only have two weeks left in New York City. I'm really going to miss my dorm at FIT and my suitemates. Well . . . most of them. Bailey and Avery have been terrific, but Madison? Not so much. I've tried to be nice, but she makes rude comments whenever she can. No matter what I do, she still acts like I don't deserve to be here. Luckily, the head designers I've worked with at Stefan Meyers don't feel the same way.

Interning has been a balancing act for sure — especially working in different departments at the same time — but I've learned so much in the six weeks I've been at Stefan Meyers. This next week is all about getting everything ready for Fashion Week! I'm still in PR with Michael, plus I'll be helping Laura, Taylor, and the sound engineer. Stefan also mentioned the chance to work with models, but he hasn't figured out the day yet.

Juggling everything has been a lot harder than I anticipated. Especially when it comes to my social life. Don't get me wrong. I didn't think I'd spend my internship just hanging out, but I thought I'd have more time to sketch and see Jake, especially since he's in school here. Instead, I've spent my days running from one department to the

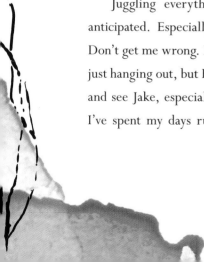

next, working late, and falling into bed exhausted at night. As for Jake? I'm just hoping we're still friends.

Everything really came to a head three days ago. I got the chance to be a guest judge on *Teen Design Diva*, the show that gave me my start. I had plans with Jake after, but filming ran late, and I couldn't even tell him because my phone died. By the time I got home and charged my phone, it was too late. I haven't spoken to Jake since. It just stinks. I know how lucky I am to have all these great opportunities, but I can't help feeling bad for hurting Jake.

On the bright side, my best friend Alex is coming to visit! She's only staying for the weekend, but at least it's something. I wish she could be here during Fashion Week too, but maybe it's for the best. The balancing act I was talking about before is sure to get a lot harder in the next two weeks, and if Alex were here during Stefan's show, I'd feel bad about not spending time with her.

I can't believe I get to be a part of Fashion Week! It's literally a dream come true. Stefan says these next two weeks "are the ones that really matter." I'm sure it will be stressful, but exciting too. And to think, I was there from start to finish.

Xoxo — Chloe

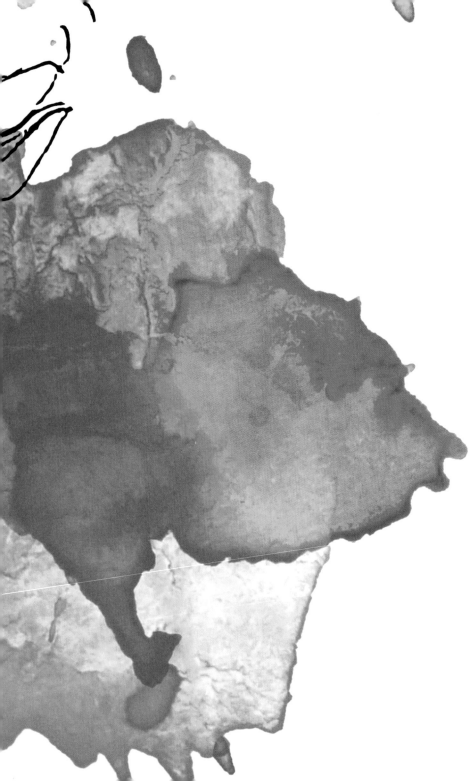

As I get dressed for work Monday morning, I try to focus on the positive. I feel ridiculous focusing on the fact that Jake and I still haven't spoken after I accidentally blew him off.

As if he read my mind, my phone buzzes with a text from Jake. "Meet for lunch to talk?"

"Definitely!" I write back. Hopefully that means he's not too mad at me.

Now that I know I have lunch plans, I go to my closet to find the perfect outfit. Today's answer comes in a graphic midi skirt in black and white, a short-sleeve black blouse, and black, multi-strap, chunky-heeled sandals. I put on my makeup, do a final once-over in front of the mirror, and am ready to take on whatever the day brings.

When I arrive at the office, Michael is waiting for me. "How goes the celebrity life?" he asks.

"Please," I say with a laugh. "It's hardly that."

"The *Design Diva* website begs to differ," he says, showing me the site on his laptop.

I glance at it and see a photo of me with a caption that says, "Meet the Surprise *Teen Design Diva* Judge." I stifle a groan. Great. That's all I need. When I first started here, Madison and some of her friends called me Diva Girl, like I was some TV star with no talent. Now it's sure to start up again. I don't want anyone thinking fame is all I want.

"Don't look so glum," says Michael. "This news puts Stefan in the spotlight even more. He was right about you judging the show. It was great publicity for the label."

"It *was* a great experience," I agree. "But I'm not running to Hollywood just yet. I'm here to serve." I do a mock bow.

"Good to hear, because we have a lot to do," says Michael.

Just then, my phone buzzes, and I do my best to keep my focus on my boss.

"We need to get gift bags for Fashion Week," Michael continues. "I have the items in bins here —"

My phone buzzes again, and this time I sneak a peek. It's Jake with a meeting place for lunch.

"Chloe?" says Michael, an edge to his voice.

I snap back to attention. "Sorry," I say sheepishly.

Michael sighs. "As I was saying, the items are in the bins, and the bags are here. Everyone will receive an iPhone cover, but the women's bags will also contain this perfume and the men's will get this cologne."

My phone buzzes again, and I can't help but look.

"Is that your paparazzi calling?" Michael asks. He's smiling but clearly annoyed. "Do you want me to leave you alone so you can talk?"

I turn off my phone. "No, sorry."

"Do you have any questions?" Michael asks.

"I got it," I say, repeating all his instructions to show that I was listening.

"Very well. I'll check in after lunch." With that, he turns and walks back to his office.

For the first time, I really take in the bins before me. There's a lot of stuff. Forcing myself to stay on task, I crouch down on the floor and start putting the bags together. I inspect the perfumes and lipstick cases, wondering if the fragrance or color would look good on me. After about fifty bags, though, my mind starts to wander, and I don't care about the colors or perfume smells. I just go through the motions.

After a while I get up to stretch and check the clock. Only an hour to go until I'm supposed to meet Jake. I hear Michael's door opening and glance at the bags before me.

STEFAN
MEYERS
PHONE
COVER

SM
GIFT BAG
Items

COLOGNE FOR MEN

PERFUME
FOR
WOMEN

I feel proud of how many I've assembled until I see the bins with cologne — they're still completely full.

I panic and check the gift bags. No! I put the same things in all of them. *This is what happens when you don't pay attention, Chloe*, I chide myself.

I quickly empty out the bags and start fixing my mistake. Thankfully, Michael's door is closed again. For the next hour, I keep my head in the game, feeling lucky I caught my mistake in time.

* * *

When I get to the café Jake suggested, I shield my eyes and scan the crowd for his face.

"Table for one?" asks a waitress.

"Um, no, I'm waiting —" I begin. Suddenly, I hear my name.

"Over here, Chloe!" Jake calls, waving his arm in the air. He's already seated at a small table, and I walk over to join him, smoothing my skirt as I take a seat.

"You look nice," he says.

"Thanks," I say, taking a nervous sip of water. "So, um, about last week . . ."

Jake takes my hand, and butterflies immediately appear in my stomach. "I was annoyed because I wanted to see you, but I know it wasn't your fault."

"It was," I say. "I should have texted you sooner — as soon as the judging thing came up. I'm really sorry. Everything has just been nuts. And with Fashion Week around the corner it's only going to get crazier."

"You're right about that," Jake agrees. "You'll have to be on hand whenever they need you."

I think about this as the waitress takes our orders. I order a muffin and tea — I don't think I can eat much more. What Jake said is true. If we had little time to see each other before, there will be even less time now. I can't spend the next two weeks being tied to my texts.

"The timing hasn't been great for us, has it?" Jake says.

I smile sadly. I know he's thinking the same thing I am. "At least we'll always have California, right?"

Jake grins. "Definitely. I'll be on the lookout for your Fashion Week designs. And I visit my dad in California a lot. We can always hang then."

Maybe romance isn't in the cards now, but I realize I've made a good friend. When you're following your dreams, that's a must.

When I get back to the office, I see several neatly stacked piles of papers sitting on top of my desk waiting for me.

"I've looked through the gift bags, and they're a go. Nice job," Michael says, walking over. "The next task requires more brain power."

"Sign me up," I say.

"It's crucial we get information about Stefan's designs out to the public," Michael explains. "I need you to call the newspapers and television networks that have agreed to interview Stefan to confirm time, place, etc. You'd be surprised how often the details get mixed up. We can't afford for that to happen."

Michael grabs a paper from the top of the stack and hands it to me — a list of contacts. I glance at the names and recognize some of them from television and red carpet shows. My mouth goes dry just thinking about calling them.

"What will I say?" I ask.

Michael seems to sense my nervousness. "Don't worry, I have that ready for you. Just follow this script," he says, handing me another piece of paper. "The schedule of events is here as well."

I relax a little. What could be easier than reading off a paper?

"Lastly," Michael continues, "I've compiled a list of fashion bloggers and journalists for you to touch base with. We want to make sure they're at the show, viewing Stefan's designs. Again, everything has been arranged, but confirmation is key. We don't want to miss these opportunities."

Michael hands me another template to follow with all the information explained. "You can do these confirmations via email. Just copy and paste the contents of this paper, changing the names as necessary. I've emailed it to you as well."

"No problem," I say, nodding and trying my best to sound confident.

Once Michael leaves, I try to get down to business, but it doesn't take long for my insecurities to take over. Over the course of my internship, I've proven time and time again that I can tackle new challenges. But apparently worrying each time a new one surfaces will never end — at least not entirely.

I give myself five minutes of freak-out time, letting all the worst-case scenarios run through my head. I could flub the script and tell someone the wrong day. I could read the wrong template. I could totally forget to call someone on the list. Someone could be rude and hang up on me.

But the more I think about the worst possibilities, the more ridiculous they seem. I mean, why would someone hang up on me? And even if that did happen, it wouldn't be the end of the world.

Focus, Chloe, I think, pushing all the craziness out of my mind.

Taking a deep breath, I make my way down the list of contacts I need to call. For each one, I follow Michael's script and consult the schedule, making sure to get all of the details right. With each call, my voice is more assertive.

The only downside, which is probably something I should have figured out earlier, is that I don't actually get to talk to any of the famous people on the list. It's an assistant — or maybe even an intern just like me — answering every call. Which, duh, makes total sense. Glamorous people are probably busy doing glamorous things.

Once I've finished confirming all of Stefan's interview dates and times, I move on to the next project. Writing emails to the bloggers and journalists is a far less nerve-racking task. At least then I don't have to worry about what to say.

I work the entire afternoon but manage to finish all confirmations. For both the calls and e-mails, I make sure to keep careful records of everyone I contacted and everyone who's replied. I roll my neck from side to side and double check my lists to make sure I left nothing out.

"Well done," says Michael when I show him my completed work. "I know Stefan promised you PR would be all about glitz and glamour, but what you've been doing is so important for the show's success. I really appreciate it."

It would have been cool to talk with someone famous, but being so involved in the process was rewarding on its own as well. And knowing that I played even a small part in a glossy print ad or *Entertainment Tonight* interview is still pretty amazing.

"Today was great. I'm just happy to be involved!" I tell him.

Michael's eyes twinkle. "Fabulous! Tomorrow, though, be prepared for a little glam."

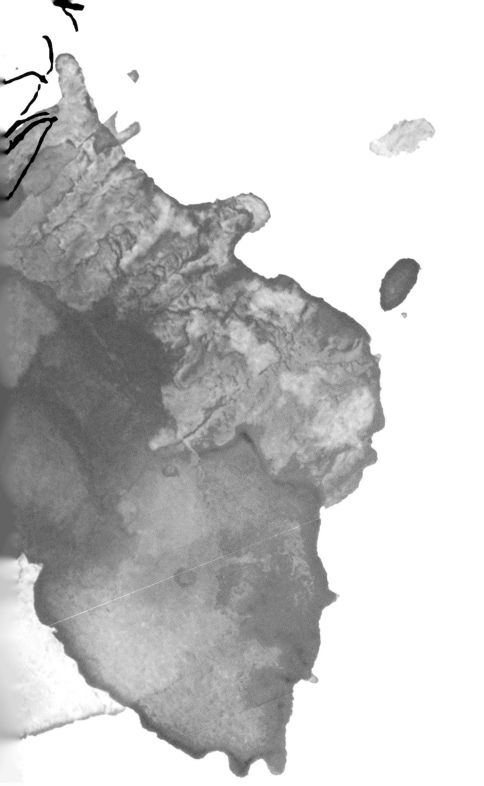

3

Tuesday morning, I'm up extra early. Michael didn't want to reveal what was on the agenda for today in case there was a last-minute change, so I'm not sure what to dress for. After several closet scans, I leave the dorm in a pair of coated brown jeans, a white blouse, gold cuff bracelet, and metallic sandals. I'm too excited to sit still on the subway, so I walk to the office, doing my best not to run.

When I get to Michael's office, he's not alone — Laura and Taylor, the head designers I've worked with — and Liesel McKay are there too. Liesel is an amazing designer in her own right, but she's also Jake's mom and my mentor from my *Teen Design Diva* days.

What are they doing here? I wonder. *I'm not supposed to see them until Thursday. Did I do something wrong? And if so, what does Liesel have to do with that? Is she here to soften the blow?*

INTERN
OUTFIT
Design

WHITE
BLOUSE

Do It All
Outfit!

GOLD
CUFF

BROWN
COATED
JEANS

METALLIC
SANDALS

Thankfully, Michael immediately puts me at ease. "Chloe, I'm glad you're here. We're doing a dry run of next week's runway show. We'll be working with the models and doing any last-minute alterations. We also need to finalize the order in which the pieces will appear. The photographers will take pictures so we can have a visual to use the day of. I need you to help with whatever they need."

I breathe a sigh of relief. Why do I always jump to the worst conclusions? Having Laura and Taylor here makes total sense. Laura's knits and the art deco designs she did with Taylor will be showcased during Fashion Week. And Liesel and Taylor were working on a project for Fashion Week too.

"When do we start?" I ask.

"About twenty minutes," says Michael. "We have a studio on the eleventh floor, and they're still setting it up. Get yourself some coffee, relax if you can."

Coffee will energize me more, but it will give me something to do. Besides, I can't risk not being fully awake!

* * *

Twenty minutes later, fully caffeinated, I follow Michael, Laura, Taylor, and Liesel upstairs to the studio. There are white sheets covering the floor and lights set up all around the room. A group of photographers is standing off to one side. As soon as we walk in, one of them walks over and extends his hand. "Jordan LeMure," he introduces himself.

I know that name! He's been interviewed on a bunch of fashion shows. "Chloe Montgomery," I say.

He smiles. "I've seen your work. That was some good television!"

I blush. "Thanks."

Just then, Laura calls out, "The models are here! Chloe, can you help get them lined up in the hall?"

"Watch for my cues to bring the models in," Jordan says before I leave. "Laura, Taylor, and Liesel will tell you which pieces each girl should be wearing."

"Got it," I say, rushing out to meet the models.

Laura hands me a list with the outfits the models will be trying on. "They will be modeling the clothes in this order," she says. "You can find all the needed items on this rack." She motions to a stand a few feet away.

The models slip into sky-high heels and line up, knowing the drill better than I do. I scan the checklist Laura gave me and pull down a short-sleeved, gray wool dress with an art deco-inspired skirt. I like the way the black and white pleating spices up the gray.

While that model is dressing, I pull down more clothes so there is minimal lag between shoots. I expect the models to give me attitude since I'm younger than them and clearly new to this, but they just smile, take the clothes, and say thank you.

As beautiful as the clothing is, it's amazing how the models make the clothing come alive. The gray wool dress, for example, is stylish on its own. However, the model's long torso draws my attention to the stretch of the fabric. When she walks, my eyes are pulled to the belt at the waist and the geometric pattern of the skirt. She stops in the center of the floor, allowing the photographers to take photos.

The next dress on my list is one I remember discussing with Laura. It's a strapless dress with blue accents and a pleated white-and-blue skirt. A model tries it on and walks toward the photographers. Her walk has a bounce to it, showing she gets the fun, flirty intent of the piece.

"One minute," I hear Jordan saying as the model finishes her shoot. "Chloe, come here, please."

I look at him like he's made a mistake, but he motions me over. "I need you to stand in for the model while we fix the lighting. Can you do that?"

"Just stand?" I ask.

"Move around a little too," Jordan says. He has me walk a few paces while the other photographers play with the lighting and check their lenses. Seeing what I have of the models, I know I'm nowhere near their level, but for these few minutes, I feel glamorous anyway.

When I'm done, I rush back to the racks and continue passing out clothes. There are two dresses left in Laura's collection before we break for lunch. I pull a short-sleeved V-neck sweater dress off the rack. The cream-colored pleated skirt pairs well with the top, which is an array of black, white, and gold lines converging.

The last piece is the lavender dress with black trim Laura designed. I'm filled with happiness as I remember her telling me that my pocket design was her inspiration for this piece. The model slips it on, and I grin as I watch the garment come to life.

As we break for lunch, the models change out of their heels and back into the flats they were wearing when they arrived. I remember the day I walked to the *Vogue* offices, feet full of blisters. My heels weren't nearly as tall as the ones these models are wearing. Their feet have to be killing them, but you wouldn't know it. They didn't complain when Jordan asked for photo retakes or had them stand perfectly still under the hot lights. It's all about making Stefan's styles a success. I need to remember that the next time I consider complaining.

GRAY
WOOL
DRESS

SM
FASHION WEEK
Designs

SWEATER
DRESS

ART DECO
PRINT

TANK
DRESS

GOLD
LINE
ACCENTS

When I get back to my dorm that night, Madison, Bailey, Avery, and I chomp on Chinese food and talk Fashion Week. "I can't wait for you guys to meet Alex on Saturday," I say. "I'm so excited for her to get here!"

"Oh, that's right," says Madison, frowning. "I forgot she was coming."

Avery waves her hand dismissively in Madison's direction. "The more the merrier. When we hang in my dorm back at school, we can cram twenty people in there to watch a movie."

"She better not be bringing an entourage with her," Madison grumbles.

"Just her," I say, then try to change the subject. "I wish she could help out with Fashion Week. I got to work with some of the models today! It was so cool!"

"I could never model," says Avery. "I'm way too shy for that."

"Plus I'm sooo not graceful," Bailey adds. "I'd probably trip on the catwalk and ruin the designs."

I laugh. "Me too! But I got to stand in for one of the models today — just for a second — and I'll admit, it was pretty cool. Intimidating, but cool."

"I'd rather see my name in lights for my designs, not for how I appear in front of a camera," Madison says snidely.

You'd have to be an idiot not to get that dig. I take a deep breath and remind myself that my stint on *Teen Design Diva* was not about fame — it was about my skill as a designer.

"Agreed," I say. "But if it weren't for models, the designs wouldn't get noticed."

Madison turns away from me and directs her question to Avery and Bailey. "Do you think we'll get to be involved in the show?"

"My cousin interned out in LA a while back and got to help out with Fashion Week there. She mostly ran around making sure all the set-up went smoothly. But she said she got to help in the back of the house getting clothing ready, dressing the models, that sort of thing too. We won't see our names in lights yet, but all this stuff is also really important."

Madison frowns. "I guess," she says, sounding unimpressed. "I was hoping to talk to celebs or something. I worked really hard in the jewelry department, *and* I helped with dresses." She turns to me. "Don't you want everyone to know which pieces you put together or which design is yours?"

I'm so surprised she's talking to me again that it takes me a minute to answer. I'm sure she's expecting me to rant about wanting all the credit I can get, and I'd be lying if I said I didn't care about that at least a little. But one thing I've learned the past six weeks is that it takes a lot of people to put something together. There are plenty of designers who've been working a lot longer than I have who deserve credit too. All our ideas together, bouncing off each other, blending into one, is what made each design work.

I open my mouth to answer, but it's obvious I took too long, because Madison rolls her eyes and says, "Oh, please. Don't even try to say you don't care about that. Everyone does!"

"Why are you always so mad?" Bailey asks Madison.

"I just think we all have to pay our dues," Madison says, giving me a pointed look. "I work hard too, and no one's said a word about what I've come up with!"

"That doesn't mean they haven't noticed," I say quietly. "The only reason —"

"Whatever," Madison interrupts. "I don't need advice from Miss Diva here." She picks up the remains of her food, throws it in the trash, and slams the door to her room.

"Oh, my gosh," says Avery. "That girl is a bottomless pit of negativity. What is her problem?"

I shake my head. "Who knows? I mean, to a certain extent, I get where she's coming from. We all want the spotlight. Waiting for it to happen can be hard."

Bailey nods. "That's true, I suppose. But it still doesn't give her the right to be so rude."

Avery, Bailey, and I finish eating and spend the rest of the night chatting and gossiping, imagining the day, years from now, when interns will be working for us.

* * *

The next morning, I'm putting the finishing touches on my outfit — a short-sleeved, black triangle dress — when my phone buzzes with a text from Michael: "Meet me at Lincoln Center."

I quickly pull my hair back with a metallic clip, grab my sketchpad, and run out the door. I'm looking forward to the twenty-minute subway ride. I haven't had nearly enough time during my internship to work on my own designs, but there's nothing like Fashion Week to inspire!

METALLIC
HAIR CLIP

INTERN
OUTFIT
Design

FLUTTER-SLEEVE
DRESS

*Love this
print!*

BLACK TRIANGLE
PATTERN

SKETCHBOOK
IN HAND
ALWAYS!

BLACK ANKLE
BOOTS

When the train arrives, I plop down in the nearest open seat and take out my sketchpad. So far most of my sketches have been of people I've seen around the city. Today, I'm thinking of some Chloe Montgomery originals. I choose a shimmery blue pencil and sketch a high-low dress that swoops to the ankles in the back and stops just above the knee at the front. I play with the idea of straps but nix them in favor of a halter neckline and keyhole opening at the bust. Suddenly, I get another idea. This could be the perfect dress for prom — my own personal version of Fashion Week!

We arrive at my stop before I know it, and I stow my sketchbook, mentally vowing to return to my design later. I hurry off the train and into Lincoln Center, where I quickly spot Michael waiting for me.

"Today we're scouting out our Fashion Week location!" he announces, sounding energized and excited. "Since Stefan's emphasis is on art deco, we want a clean, white tent. Anything too over-the-top will distract from the designs."

Michael cups his hands around his eyes like he's going to take a picture and steps back, trying to visualize the area from all angles. "This," he says, motioning to the sides, "is where the audience will sit. The runway will flow down the middle."

I picture what he's describing — models walking down the runway, an opening at the back of the runway from which they'll enter, chairs on either side, everything in white, maybe little white lights on the ceiling.

"It needs something," says Michael. "Like a centerpiece of some kind."

I play the show in my mind. Models wearing Taylor and Liesel's art deco designs strut down the runway. One is wearing a satin gown embroidered with overlapping Vs. Another showcases a floor-length gown of shimmering silver satin. Dresses with light beading and fringe with metallic threading parade in my head. I remember the press release I worked on with Michael — "Stefan Meyers Brings Back Roaring Twenties with Elegant Art Deco." Whatever we add has to be grand but not take away from the designs.

"How about an enormous chandelier at the end of the runway?" I suggest, imagining light ricocheting off the crystals and illuminating the metallic threading on the dresses. "That would really add some drama and glamour. We could do something reminiscent of the 1920s."

Michael closes his eyes. "That will be perfect! The bee's knees, some might say! Just like you, my dear."

DRESS
DEVELOPMENT
Sketches

Sleek draped halter

♡the high low!↓

Bows Bows +more Bows! ♡

high halter

✓Striped Bodice

Dramatic Balgown Skirt ↓

Keyhole halter→

Belt↗

✓♡shaped Beaded neckline

Drapey off-sh. Cowl neck.

Beaded Waist →

Triangle halter

tulle↙

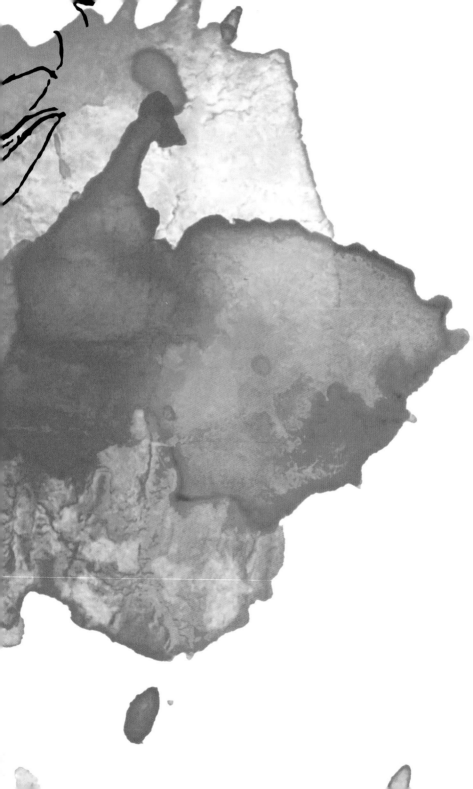

On Thursday I'm back with Laura and Taylor. As soon as I arrive, they wheel out racks of clothes that will be used in next week's show. I saw some of the designs during the model fitting, but things were moving so quickly, I didn't pay attention to every garment. Now I take a closer look and am thrilled to see some items I worked on during my internship.

"The show is Wednesday, so we're down to the wire," says Laura. "We'll need your help getting these ready and packaged away. Everything needs to be steamed."

Taylor wheels out a machine and tells me the dos and don'ts — mainly how not to burn myself or ruin the clothes. Then she fills the machine with water and runs the handheld attachment over the garments. All wrinkles disappear.

"Practice on these first," Taylor says, pointing to a pile of clothes.

I pick up the steamer and slowly go over the clothes. The water drips on a few of the pieces, but after a couple tries I get the hang of it.

"There are forty pieces here," says Laura. "Take your time. If you need us, we're only a shout away."

They leave, and I do a few more practice steaming runs before moving on to the Fashion Week items. Steaming may not be glamorous, but it's surprisingly relaxing. It's also really gratifying watching tiny wrinkles disappear and seeing the clothes come out looking like new.

I spot the flowered pockets and denim designs, along with the art deco sweater dress I worked on with Laura. I remember discussing how great the dress would look with a geometric pattern and metallic threading. Seeing the finished piece is like a dream come true.

The silk dresses I worked on with Taylor are there too, and I remember the sketches I drew for her. I find the dressy jackets I helped Laura design and hold them up to the dresses. The shawl collars in silk and velvet complement Taylor's floor-length gowns. Another jacket, lightly embroidered with pearls, helps bring out the pearl embellishments on one of Taylor's art deco dresses.

I smile to myself as I steam. There won't be a place in the program that says, "Chloe helped with these," but I'll know. And for now, that's enough.

* * *

After lunch, Laura and Taylor stop by to examine my work.

"Nice job," says Laura. "My first time steaming, I ruined five dresses."

"I only ruined two," Taylor brags.

Laura shoots her a knowing look. "I wouldn't get cocky. If I remember correctly, most of the stuff you steamed was dripping wet. It took days to salvage it."

Taylor scowls. "Maybe. But it *was* salvaged."

"Barely," Laura mumbles.

I stare at them. Their competitiveness kind of reminds me of the rivalry I have with Nina LeFleur, a girl from back home. The only difference is that Laura and Taylor seem to like each other too. "Where do I go next?" I ask, trying to diffuse the argument.

Taylor checks her watch. "Stefan wants you to see what sound editing is all about. Gary, the sound engineer, is the brains behind the music for Fashion Week."

"His studio is on the ninth floor," says Laura. "I'll take you there."

SWEATER DRESS

PEARL DETAILS

FLOWER POCKET JEANS

METALLIC THREAD

BIAS-CUT SILK DRESS

Art Deco-Inspired SM Designs

FASHION WEEK *Designs*

VELVET SHAWL COLLAR

SILK BIAS-CUT GOWN

COLLARLESS NECKLINE

SILK GOWN WITH PEARL "DOTS"!

PLEATED DROP-WAIST SKIRT

When we arrive on the ninth floor, a guy wearing a white button-down over dark blue jeans greets us. "I'm Gary," he says, tipping his black derby hat.

"Chloe," I say, extending my hand.

"Take good care of her," Laura says before heading off.

"I'm working on the music the models will be walking to," Gary explains as we head to his studio. "I'm thinking something fun and dance-centric." He plays a few samples and has me walk to the music. I feel a little silly and wonder if he's making fun of me, but when I peek at his face, I see that he's deep in concentration, fidgeting with the dials and changing the speed and songs.

To be honest, I don't usually pay attention to the songs used on the runway. All I focus on are the designs. It makes me wish Alex were already here — music is so her thing.

Gary plays with the dials, switches tunes, and writes something down. He does this a few more times before taking a break. "What do you think?" he asks.

I'm not a music expert, but I like the beat. "The rhythm is good," I offer.

Gary nods. "Good. I think so too," he says.

"Do you like being behind the scenes like this?" I ask. As soon as the words are out, I put my hand over my mouth. That sounded kind of rude.

Thankfully, Gary just smiles. "You mean not getting the spotlight?" He shrugs. "It bugged me when I started out. Reviewers rarely, if ever, mention the songs. But it's cool. I've been doing this for years now, and I love watching the impact the right songs have on the show."

He has a point, I realize. I might not have noticed the songs in the past, but I imagine a fashion show without music — it would be dead and boring.

"I work for a variety of designers and do films too," Gary continues, "but there's something about Fashion Week. There's nothing like that immediate thrill of watching an audience react to the shows. Yeah, it's totally about the designs, but I sometimes see people tapping their feet to the music. It reminds me how important this job is."

I nod. I'm glad Stefan had me spend the afternoon here. It's a perfect reminder of how much goes into a successful fashion show — every step, no matter how small, counts.

Gary and I spend the rest of day listening to music and testing out songs. By the end of the day, he has a selection ready to go.

"Wow," I say as he packs up, "that's a lot of work for a show that's only fifteen minutes long."

Gary smiles. "You remember that next week. Not everyone wants the spotlight, Chloe. You can have credit without lights shining on your face."

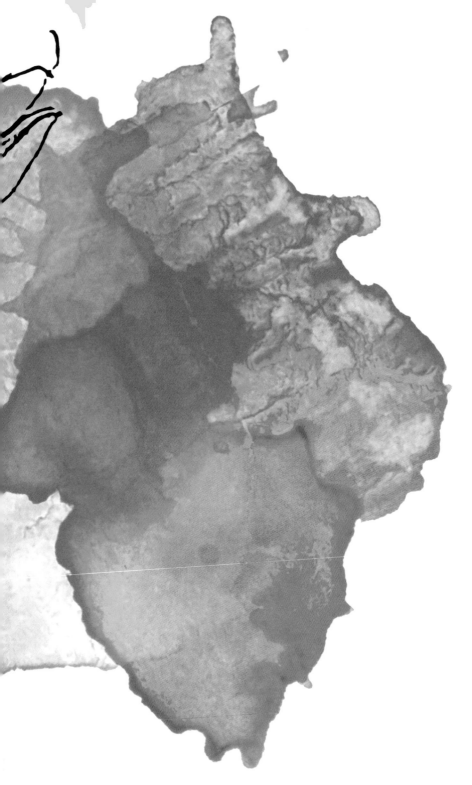

When the weekend finally arrives, I wait impatiently for Alex. Her last text, "Leaving airport now!" was an hour ago. How far is the airport, anyway? Darn New York traffic.

When the taxi finally pulls up in front of my dorm, I rush out to meet it. It's been two months since I've seen Alex, and I miss my best friend so much. She clearly feels the same way, because she already has one foot out the door before the cab has even come to a complete stop.

We throw our arms around each other as we jump and screech. The taxi driver honks his horn and reminds Alex to pay him. "Oops," she says, quickly handing him a wad of cash. Then we get back to yelling and hugging.

I take a step back and see how much Alex has changed. "What happened?" I say, noticing her highlights, makeup, and new outfit — a fitted black T-shirt, distressed boyfriend jeans, and studded black flats. She still looks like the same old Alex, just a much chicer version.

Alex grins and twirls. "You can't have a best friend living the high life and not have that rub off on you. I've been reading fashion blogs and trying to find stuff that is stylish but still feels like me. I wanted to surprise you. You like?"

"Definitely," I say. "Does this mean we can shop together now?" My eyes glaze over as I envision hours of store hopping with Alex. "We have years to make up for!"

"Hold up," says Alex, grimacing a little. "Baby steps. You're making me want to crawl back into sweats."

"Please, no!" I say in mock horror. "Not that!"

Alex laughs, and it reminds me again how happy I am to have my friend here. I wish she could stay longer so I could really show her around NYC, but two days is better than nothing. We quickly take her suitcase up to my room and head over to Bryant Park.

"How do you deal with all these people?" Alex asks as we get jostled on the busy streets.

I shrug. "It doesn't bother me anymore. I actually love it. I'm afraid Santa Cruz's silence will kill me when I get back."

"Don't worry," says Alex, putting her arm around me. "I'll stand outside your window and bang drums all night to make the transition easier."

"Ha! Speaking of home, what have I missed?" I ask. Since I started my internship, there hasn't been much time to gossip with Alex. There's so much I want to talk about. None of it is earth-shattering, but when you're talking to your best friend, it feels like everything is.

Alex fills me in on Nina and her groupies. Turns out Nina has less of an entourage than she did when I left. Apparently, after watching us on *Teen Design Diva*, there's a bit of a divide between Team Nina and Team Chloe.

"I kid you not," Alex says when I look at her in disbelief. "Be prepared to have your own groupies upon your return."

"Just what I need," I say, rolling my eyes. But then I get an idea on how to make good with this ridiculous news. "Maybe they'd want to learn designing and all that. Then they can do it themselves and lay off the hero worship."

"Good luck with that," Alex says as we walk into the park. We sit in the games section and choose a table with Jenga. "So, tell me what's going on with Jake. You've hardly said a word about him lately."

"I figured it would be easier to talk to you about it in person," I say, pulling a wooden piece from the Jenga tower. "He's a really nice guy, and he's so cute, but I have so much going on right now. It's been almost impossible to make time for him. And then when we did make plans, I'd have to cancel. The day of *Teen Design Diva* judging was the worst.

My phone died, so I couldn't tell him I was running late." I frown, still feeling bad about that day.

Alex smiles sympathetically. "That must have been hard for both of you." She pulls a wooden block, and the tower wobbles but doesn't fall.

I nod. "It was. Trying to hang out was too much pressure."

"I'm sorry," says Alex. "I know you really liked him."

"I still do, but it's not like I won't see him again. Besides, boyfriends are drama. Friends always stay." I gently push a loose block from the bottom and stack it beside Alex's piece.

Alex blushes and fiddles with the tab on her soda. "So, um, boyfriends can be drama, but I sort of have one. His name is Dan," she says.

I'm so surprised by her announcement that I almost knock over the blocks. "Why didn't you tell me?"

"It wasn't official until last week, and then I figured I might as well wait and tell you in person," she says. "Are you upset, since you and Jake . . ." Her voice trails off.

I roll my eyes. "Oh my gosh! I told you, I'm fine. Really. Now spill."

"Well," Alex says, pulling a block and causing the tower to wobble, "he likes basketball, just like me. And we've gone hiking a lot."

"Do you make him watch bad reality television with you?" I ask jokingly. I pull a block, and the tower tumbles to the table.

"Nah, that's *our* special thing," Alex says, pointing at me. "But we do scarf Doritos and pizza together."

I laugh. "A match made in heaven. I'm really happy for you."

Alex and I wander around a bit more, even acting silly and riding the carousel. It's mostly full of kids, but people smile at us as we park ourselves on a horse and zebra. We grin as the animals go up and down. Being chic intern Chloe has been great, but I've missed being goofy with Alex.

"Two days is not enough to spend with you at all!" I say as we head back to my dorm. "I wish you could stay and help with Fashion Week."

Alex grins mischievously. "That's actually something I wanted to talk to you about. I did some research, and I think there might be a way I can stay longer . . ."

* * *

We hurry back to the dorm to run Alex's plan by Avery and Bailey. I'm less excited, however, to see the look on Madison's face when I suggest Alex should stay longer.

"Guys," I say as we walk in, "this is my best friend, Alex."

"Hey!" says Avery. "Nice to meet you! I love your jeans!"

"And your shoes — super cute!" Bailey adds.

Alex grins and blushes. "Thanks!"

Madison just sits there quietly. I've told Alex all about Madison in our calls and texts, so hopefully the silence isn't a surprise.

Alex gives me a little nod, and I launch into her plan. "So I know Alex is only supposed to be staying two days, but we, uh, wondered if you guys would mind if she stayed a little longer." I pause. "Like maybe until Stefan's fashion show is done? Wednesday?"

I expect Bailey, Avery, and Madison to at least want to discuss it, but Avery just shrugs. "Fine by me. I told you this suite is roomy compared to what I'm used to."

"Same here," says Bailey. "We're always in and out anyway. Mallory Kane's show is tomorrow, so I won't be here a good part of the day."

"And Thomas Lord is Thursday," Avery adds, "so I'll probably be gone helping with some sort of prep on Monday and Tuesday."

Madison sighs and rolls her eyes. "Whatever. But she's going to be pretty bored while you're at work."

"Well, I've been doing research," says Alex, "and a lot of the Fashion Week websites I've looked at say designers are always looking for more volunteers. Is that true?"

Avery claps her hands. "Totally true! What an awesome idea! Why didn't I think of that earlier?"

"Do you think it'll be hard to clear with Stefan?" I ask.

"Doubt it," says Bailey, "but I'd ask first thing Monday morning. Don't wait until Wednesday."

Alex and I hug. "This will be so cool," I say. Then a thought comes to me. "But what about your plane ticket?"

"My dad made it open-ended. Once this is cleared, I'll call him, and he can confirm the departure date. Surprise!"

"I'm so jealous," says Avery, fake pouting. "I wish I'd thought of having a friend volunteer with me."

"It was all Alex's idea," I say with a grin. I'm so excited for her to see my designs and the world I've been living in for the past two months. Finally, I can share it with my best friend.

7

Alex and I are up extra early Monday morning, and I'm surprised by how excited my best friend is to put together her outfit. She pulls out a patterned V-neck blouse and pairs it with loose black shorts. Metallic sandals complete the look.

I'm impressed. "I'm still surprised by this new Alex, but I so love it!"

Alex twirls in front of the mirror and bows dramatically. "Why, thank you, darling!"

I'd been thinking of wearing black shorts too, but don't want us looking like twins, so instead I choose a short-sleeve lace blouse and pair it with taupe silk shorts and open-toed flats.

CHLOE'S OUTFIT
Design

Casually
Elegant

SHORT-SLEEVE
LACE TOP

TAUPE SILK
SHORTS

Best friend
& internship
in one day!

FAVORITE
FLAT SANDALS

"I can't wait to see where you work," Alex says as we leave the dorm. "Let's just hope Stefan is looking for volunteers. Maybe I should stay hidden until he says it's okay."

"Sounds like a plan," I say. I try to sound confident, but butterflies form in my stomach. What if he says no? We have almost an hour before the meeting starts. That will give Alex and me plenty of time to get to work and talk with Stefan, but that still doesn't totally quiet my butterflies.

* * *

When we get to the office, Stefan is setting up the meeting room. Alex hides behind the door, and I walk into the conference room.

"Early and eager," says Stefan, smiling. "I like that in an intern."

"Do you need help?" I ask.

"Why not? Please place a packet at everyone's seat," Stefan says, handing me a stack of papers.

I do as he says, but the butterflies are getting worse. "Um, Mr. Meyers?" I finally manage. "I was hoping to talk with you about something."

Stefan stops organizing and gives me his full attention. "What is it?" His face is serious.

"My friend Alex is visiting, and we were wondering if you could use more Fashion Week volunteers," I say. My heart is pounding, and I wring my fingers as I wait for him to answer.

Stefan breaks into a grin. "Is that all? I thought you were going to bail on me. We can always use more volunteers. I'm going over a lot of info at today's meeting. Can she get here?"

My face reddens. "Um . . . she's waiting outside."

Stefan laughs and peers out the door. "Ah, I see her. She's not a great hider, but at least she has style." He waves Alex into the room and extends his hand. "Stefan Meyers."

"Alex," she says. "I'm so excited to be here. Thank you for letting me help."

"If you're anything like your friend Chloe," says Stefan, "this will work out perfectly."

Alex and I finish passing out the packets as interns from all departments begin trickling in. When everyone is seated, Stefan begins his speech. "Tomorrow, I, along with the rest of the designers, will be busy with last-minute Fashion Week prep, so today is our last chance to talk at length before Wednesday's show," he says.

I nudge Alex with my elbow. She grins. I know we're both jumping up and down on the inside.

Stefan starts off with a map of Lincoln Center and focuses on where our tent will be. Then he assigns our positions before, during, and after the show. Alex and I are responsible for placing the programs and gift bags on everyone's seats before the show begins. We'll also be assisting backstage with the models. I try to focus on what Stefan is saying even though my brain is turning cartwheels.

"Finally," he says, "a reminder. Your job is to assist with the Stefan Meyers brand. This is *not* a networking opportunity. This is *not* a time to tell other designers, editors, and critics how hard you've been working for me and which button was your design." He pauses and looks around the room. Is it my imagination, or do his eyes linger on Madison? "Believe me, I see your efforts. If you do what I ask of you, I'll notice. Questions?"

No one raises a hand.

"Excellent," Stefan says. "I expect to see you all at the tent by seven a.m. Wednesday. Remember to wear black, and don't forget to read through your packets. They also have your volunteer badges."

There are a few quiet groans about the early morning and the black. I don't know what the problem is. Early mornings are old news, and as for the black, it could be worse. Besides, it's Fashion Week! If Stefan said to wear a clown suit, I'd do it without complaints.

"Where to now?" asks Alex. "Can we scope out the tent for Wednesday?"

"Good idea," I say. As we get closer to Lincoln Center, the crowds thicken. Alex and I look at our maps and find Stefan's tent.

"Michael's description of it sounded great. I can't wait to see it!" I say as we duck inside. It's even better than I imagined. The white is simple yet elegant, and there's a humongous chandelier at the end of the runway, just like we'd discussed.

Alex whistles, impressed. "I love it. I was scared it would look crazy like some of those shows we watched online. Wasn't there a seal in one of them?"

I laugh. "Definitely no animals here."

We do a small tour of the space and check out the backstage area. "I can't believe we'll be a part of all this," says Alex.

"I know," I say. "I feel like I should pinch myself. I can't believe it's finally here."

* * *

That evening, Bailey tells us all about Mallory Kane's show. "It was super hectic," she says, "but amazing. I loved organizing all the outfits for the models and checking the guest list."

"I can't wait until Thursday's show!" Avery says.

"The end was really cool too," Bailey continues. "Mallory walked onstage after the last set of models, and everyone applauded. I was backstage, but all that energy was contagious. Even when I was cleaning up and packing up the clothes and extra gift bags and programs, I was so pumped. I just felt so good to be a part of the experience."

"That sounds amazing," I say. I close my eyes, picturing the lights and clothes on the runway.

"But we're not *really* a part of the experience," Madison says, cutting into my daydream.

"What do you mean?" asks Bailey.

Madison rolls her eyes. "I mean, we're just interns. You should have heard Stefan's speech this morning. He went on and on about how we need to focus on the Stefan Meyers brand. It's not about 'networking.'"

Bailey sighs. Her annoyed expression tells me she's had these conversations with Madison before. "You're there to help, not network. All the designers feel the same way about that. If you're being professional, you're asked to come back. Designers introduce themselves to you. There are opportunities."

"What do you think, Chloe?" Madison asks.

I glance back and forth between Bailey and Madison, not sure how to respond. I know if I agree with Madison, she might finally warm up to me. Although, the internship is almost over, so what does it matter? In a way, she has a point. I mean, who wouldn't want to talk to a famous designer or be the Cinderella of fashion?

But then I remember what Liesel and Laura said about things happening in their own time. I remember Gary saying there are more important things than seeing your name in lights. The truth is, regardless of how nice it would be to be the star of the show, tomorrow is about Stefan's brand and being a team player.

"I think our job is to just follow Stefan's directions," I finally say. "I wouldn't want to miss something important and be responsible for Stefan's show tanking."

Madison frowns. "Figures you wouldn't care about being heard, Diva Girl. You already had your moment in the spotlight."

"Hey!" says Alex. "Chloe worked really hard to get here."

"Forget it," I whisper.

Alex sputters like she wants to say something else but settles for glaring at Madison.

Madison gets up and heads to her room. "You guys do what you want, but I worked too hard to be a wallflower. I'm not just going to sit back." She walks to her room, then turns around one last time. "Maybe I just want this more than the rest of you."

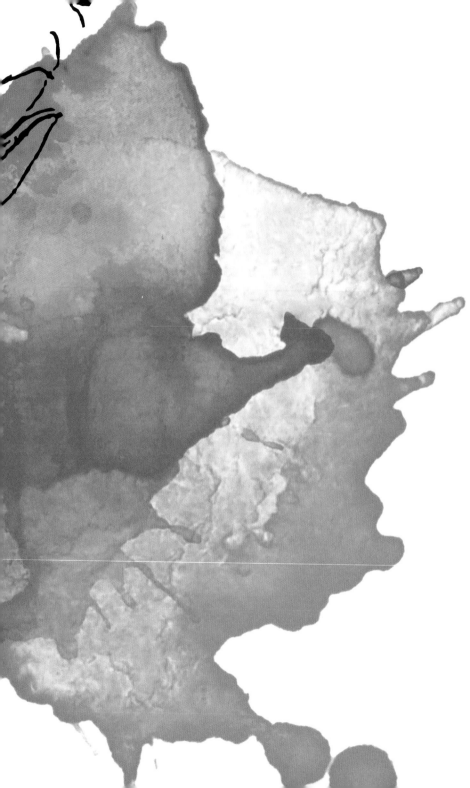

As soon as my alarm buzzes at six o'clock Wednesday morning, I jump out of bed. Alex, on the other hand, pulls the covers over her head and groans. That means I get the shower first, which is fine by me.

I quickly wash my hair and am finishing putting on my Fashion Week outfit — a black sheath dress, black tights patterned with geometric shapes (a nod to art deco), and black flats — when Alex starts banging on the door.

"Chill," I say, coming out. "I'm moving as fast as I can."

"Not my fault I can't function before eight. And factor in jet lag . . ." Eyes still half-closed, Alex pushes past me into the bathroom.

While she showers, I focus on doing my hair. I may not be able to spice up my wardrobe with some sparkle, but at

65

least I can style my hair. I blow-dry it straight, and glance at the time on my phone — six-thirty. Good thing Alex's hair is shorter than mine and will require less styling, or we'd be late for sure.

When Alex finally emerges, she's wearing black flats too, but her black shift dress and black tights with a zigzag pattern keep us from looking identical.

"You look great!" I say, checking the time again.

Alex follows my gaze and pulls her hair back into a quick bun. "Not to worry," she says. "No dryer needed."

I smile, relaxing, and hook my arm through hers as we head out the door.

* * *

We get to Lincoln Center with five minutes to spare. Stefan has even set up an area with food and coffee.

"He's, like, the best boss ever," Alex chirps, helping herself to a bagel, eggs, bacon, and coffee.

I do the same, adding some fruit to my plate as well. It's going to be a long day, so I make sure to toss a couple protein bars and fruit in my bag for later.

I look around the room at the sea of black. Even with everyone dressed in the same color, it's amazing how much individuality there is. There are dresses with lace and ribbed and patterned tights. I see a few peplum dresses too, and spot one intern wearing a long black maxi, which I love. I could picture it spiced up with a statement necklace or scarf.

Stefan raises his hand for attention. "This is it," he says. "This is what we've been working toward. We're all here for the same purpose — to make sure the show runs smoothly."

Alex and I glance at Madison, but she appears to be very focused on her bagel.

"Work hard, have a good time. Any questions?" Stefan asks. The group is silent. "No? Then onward!"

Alex and I get right to work, grabbing a cart and loading the gift bags and programs onto it. My best friend and Fashion Week — what more could a girl ask for?

* * *

Alex and I place a program and gift bag on each seat in the tent, then step back to admire the whole thing once more. Even though we saw the finished product yesterday, it's more impressive today because of the energy. Volunteers are rushing from one station to another, Gary is doing sound checks, and models are being prepped.

"Girls," says Laura, rushing toward us. She's out of breath, as usual. "If you're done here, I need you backstage assisting with the models."

FASHION
WEEK
Outfits

CHLOE'S OUTFIT

BLACK
SHIFT

BLACK
SHEATH
DRESS

ZIG-ZAG
TIGHTS

GRAPHIC
SHAPE
ACCENTS

BLACK
FLATS!

OPAQUE
TIGHTS

ALEX'S OUTFIT

Alex and I exchange an excited look and follow Laura backstage into the chaos. Hairspray is being sprayed everywhere, shoes are being thrown from one direction to another, and stylists are doing last-minute dress adjustments.

"Where do you need us?" I ask.

"You'll help dress the models and keep track of the looks," says Laura. She hands us photos of the outfits the models will wear, along with the order they go in. "We have fifteen models and thirty looks. Each model will showcase two designs. You'll notice the first model will wear the first and last design on the list. There will be some time to change looks, but we need you girls to make the changes go as quickly as possible. If you need anything, ask the stylists, okay?"

We nod, and Laura runs off to assist someone else in need.

"Ten minutes!" a familiar voice yells.

I turn and spot Liesel off to the side. She's busy making last-minute adjustments to the pieces she and Taylor collaborated on. "Liesel!" I shout, running over to give her a hug.

She pauses long enough to hug me back. "This is it, Chloe! Are you ready?" she asks.

"Born ready," I say, chuckling. "You remember Alex, right?"

"Of course. Nice to see you again," says Liesel. "Excited to be here?"

"Totally! I can't believe I get to do this!" says Alex.

Liesel grins. "Me neither. It never gets old. We'll catch up after the show, okay? Best of luck!"

Liesel rushes toward Taylor and Stefan, who have just appeared backstage, and I help the first model into her outfit. It's the lavender dress with black trim that Laura designed based on my pockets.

"I love this one," says Alex, helping a model with a crochet tank dress. I recognize the scalloped hem and metallic threading.

"I helped Laura design that one," I say.

Alex whistles. "Mighty impressive, girl."

"Five minutes!" someone calls, and Alex and I stop chatting and focus on the task at hand.

I feel my heart beating quickly as the first models line up. We add pieces of adhesive tape and pins for last-minute fixes, and then they're ready. The music starts, and it's go time. This is it. It's happening.

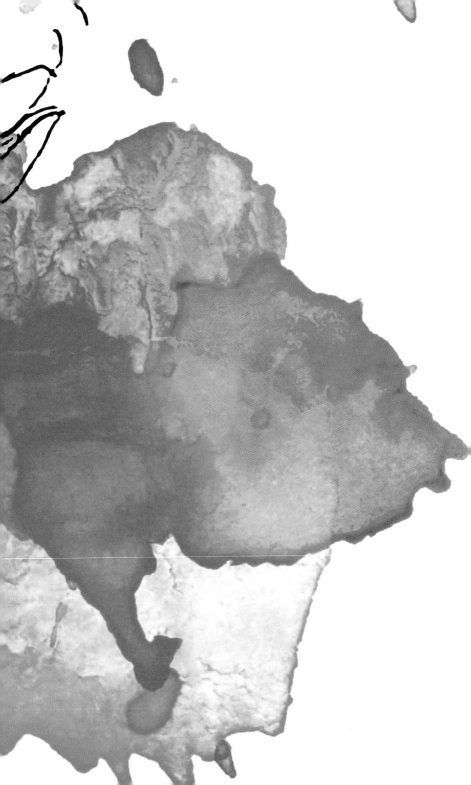

As the models hit the runway, Alex and I stay busy in the back, constantly checking Laura's list and comparing it with who's lined up to go. We have to make sure there isn't any lag time between one model and the next. That could throw off the whole show.

Even though I can't see the models on the runway, there's something amazing about seeing the designs on them backstage. The way fabric skims the hips or lays on the collarbone changes the garment, and I realize more than ever that there's a level of precision to choosing the right model to perfectly showcase a design.

It feels like we've been standing forever, and Alex and I make the mistake of sitting down just as the first models are strutting back in.

"Ladies!" yells Taylor. "Look alive!"

We jump up and rush to the models. The first fifteen looks were various knits and denims, and the last fifteen are all art deco themed. These are the pieces I've worked on with both Taylor and Laura.

A model lines up in a flowing, pleated yellow skirt and strapless bodice with shimmering geometric lines and metallic threading. I remember this design from my time with Taylor. I notice she's carrying a clam-shaped bag with white tile beads. That's the design I drew for Taylor! I remember her saying she'd pass it on to Stefan. Looks like he liked it. This is unreal. It's all I can do to focus and not scream with joy.

We move quickly, readying one design after the next. I smooth a jacket with a notched collar and beading that I recognize from my time with Laura. It fits beautifully over a satin gown embroidered with an overlapping V pattern that I helped Taylor with.

I scan the photos and list and see we're nearing the end. The dresses Liesel and Taylor worked on together are next. I help a model into a silk bias-cut gown, and a stylist adds a long pearl-tasseled necklace. I see Liesel putting the finishing touches on another model and give her a quick thumbs-up.

Out of the corner of my eye, I see Alex zipping a model into a rose-colored floor-length gown. The model

FINAL
FASHION WEEK
Design

BEADED
HEADBAND

FLOWY
PLEATED
SKIRT

BEADED &
CRYSTAL BODICE

ART DECO
BEADED
BAG

twirls in the delicate chiffon, and I notice the beading and sequin embellishments across the boat neckline. The dress is a lovely blend of vintage and glamour, and the embellishments perfectly capture the art deco vibe Stefan was going for with these pieces.

The model struts onto the runway. As breathtaking as the dress looked seconds ago, it's even better now. The chiffon flows behind the model, and the beading shimmers under the bright lights. The garment almost seems to come alive as the model floats down the catwalk.

"What do you think the chances are of us getting free samples of some of this stuff?" Alex asks as we put the next outfit on the model.

I laugh. "Doubtful — highly doubtful. It's a nice dream, though. I'd especially love this one," I say as I finish helping a model into a simple black satin dress with an art deco-inspired sash belt. I peer closer at the intricate pearl, crystal, and rhinestone detailing.

"Liesel is so skilled," says Alex. "No wonder she was a *Design Diva* winner! This will be you one day." She pokes me in the side.

"Here's hoping," I say, fastening the belt clasp.

I look at my list. One design left, and it's a total showstopper. I help the model into the silver beaded dress with a deep V-neck. The dress is held up by illusion-netting straps, giving it an ethereal look. The intricate beading design showcases Liesel's attention to detail. Unlike some of the other looks, this model's hair is pulled back in a bun, which adds to the style's sophistication. She walks onto the runway, the slinky dress hugging her hips.

Alex and I watch as the dress catches the light from the chandelier, eliciting gasps from the audience. I wipe a tear from my eye, and Alex pats my shoulder. "I feel like such an idiot for crying," I say. "This has just been such an amazing experience, and I can't believe it's almost over."

"I know. Getting to do this with you today was amazing. It makes me want to learn more about fashion too. You can really feel the dedication of all the designers today," says Alex. Her voice breaks, and she giggles. "Man, now you got me emotional. About clothes! Speak of this to no one."

I laugh. "Cross my heart."

The audience applauds for the final dress, and the model makes her return trip down the runway, heading toward the backstage area.

Now it's Stefan's turn to hit the catwalk. He has so much to be proud of today, but he's so humble as he walks out and waves to the audience, taking his time shaking their hands. He takes a final bow, and some of the audience members give him a standing ovation. As he makes his way off the stage, I see him wipe his eyes too.

BEADED
COLLAR

PEARL TASSEL
NECKLACE

BEADED
BOATNECK
GOWN

ART DECO PATTERN

ROSE-COLORED
CHIFFON GOWN

SM
FASHION WEEK
Designs

BLACK SATIN
GOWN

ILLUSION
NETTING
TOP

EMBELLISHED
WITH PEARLS,
STONES, &
SEQUINS

SILVER
BEADED
GOWN

BIAS-CUT
SKIRT

Still riding high after the end of show, Alex and I leave the backstage area to see if help is needed out front. Some interns are picking up stray programs and gift bags, and we do the same. In the distance, I see Madison sitting by herself, head in her hands, shoulders shaking. She can't be this emotional over the fashion show, can she?

I poke Alex and nod in Madison's direction. "Do you think something happened?"

Alex shrugs and shakes her head. "Who knows? That girl is all drama."

I'm mentally debating whether or not I should check on her when I hear a familiar voice yelling my name. I turn and see Jake hurrying toward me with a huge grin on his face.

"Hi!" I say, giving him a hug. It's been more than a week and a half since I last saw him, and I've missed him.

"Those designs were incredible," he says. "It must have been amazing seeing the final product after all the work you put in."

"It really was!" I say. "And the energy in the room was electrifying."

"I know!" Jake agrees. "My mom got me a ticket, so I got to sit out front and watch the whole thing. I so lucked out." He waves Liesel over and puts his arm around her.

"I loved your designs," I say to Liesel. "The last piece was phenomenal."

Liesel smiles modestly. "Thank you. It was my favorite as well. And I'm so grateful to you and Alex for your help backstage. We couldn't have done it without you."

"Hey there," Jake says as Alex walks over. "I thought you looked familiar. Chloe's best friend from California, right? Good to see you again."

The three of them recap the show, and Alex gushes about the great time she had. I take it all in, trying not to think about how much I'll miss both Jake and Liesel when I head back to California this weekend.

Suddenly, I feel everyone staring at me. "Sorry, what? I zoned out."

Liesel smiles. "We were just saying how glad we were to have spent these months with you. We'll miss you."

"Me too," I say, my eyes tearing up again.

"Don't worry," says Alex, throwing her arm around me. "I'll take care of her."

"And I'll be in Santa Cruz next month visiting my dad," says Jake. "I'll give you a call and we'll hang out?"

"You better," I say. I hug him and Liesel one last time, then Alex and I finish cleaning up and head back to the dorms, leaving the glam of Fashion Week behind.

* * *

As soon as Alex and I walk in the door, Bailey is on us. "How was the show? I've been dying to hear how it went."

"The best!" I say. "It was so cool seeing all the designs, especially the ones I got to help out with."

"I'm so excited for Thomas Lord's show tomorrow," Avery adds from where she's sitting. "But I'll be honest, I'm getting kind of sad too. Our time here is almost over. At least there's still the send-off."

I perk up. "Send-off?"

"Oh, yeah," says Bailey. "Most of the designers do a big breakfast on the last day for the interns. The lead designer comes and thanks everyone for all their hard work. Sometimes they even give you a gift."

"See?" says Alex. "I told you freebies were a possibility! And now that you have something to look forward to, you don't have to be gloomy after I leave." She winks at me.

I give her a half-hearted smile. "Too bad you can't be here for that," I say. Her flight back to California leaves tomorrow, and my last day as an intern is Friday.

Alex shrugs. "It's fine. This has been really exciting, and I wouldn't trade it for anything. I totally get why you love it here, but I'm really a Santa Cruz girl at heart. I don't think I can do the hustle and bustle thing on a daily basis."

"I can sympathize with that," says Bailey. "I miss my home in Florida too."

"Not me," says Avery, grinning. "My home is right here."

Alex throws a pillow at her and laughs.

"Hey," I say, just realizing Madison is MIA, "do you know where Madison is? I saw her crying at Fashion Week."

Avery and Bailey exchange glances. "She *really* wanted to get noticed," Avery finally says with a shrug.

"What does that mean?" I ask. "What happened?"

"She tried to show Daphne Appell, that reality show host, some of her designs, and Daphne got annoyed. I guess her people complained to Stefan. It seems like it got blown out of proportion, at least according to Madison," says Bailey, sounding like she feels bad for even relating the story. "She was here earlier and said Stefan told her she can come to the breakfast Friday, but she can't intern for him again."

"Wow," says Alex. "If I were her, I wouldn't feel right going to the breakfast."

Avery grimaces. "She won't. She's too embarrassed. She wants to change her ticket and leave Thursday."

Suddenly, the door bursts open, and we jump. It's Madison, her face red and puffy. "Hi," she says quietly.

We look at her, unsure what to say.

Madison sighs. "I'm sure you guys told Miss Diva everything?"

"I'm really sorry," I say.

Madison snorts. "Yeah, well. Me too."

No one seems to know what to say, so Alex starts packing. The rest of us — except for Madison — try to help.

Finally, I can't take the awkwardness anymore. "You should stay until Friday," I finally say, breaking the silence. "Come to the breakfast. It was just a mistake."

Madison whips her head around, and I brace myself for some of her usual bad attitude, but she deflates. "It was a big one. I just — I just wanted someone to see my designs."

I nod. We all understand wanting recognition.

"Nothing I can do about it now," Madison says, heading to her room. "So I might as well go home. But I'll say this, Diva Girl, one day you'll see my name plastered everywhere." She gives us a small, determined smile and disappears into her room to pack.

I hope I do, I think. *I hope I see all our names plastered everywhere one day.*

With Alex and Madison gone, Bailey, Avery, and I spend Thursday night packing. That way we can enjoy our last day and not feel pressured to get everything done before we leave Saturday.

And yet, when I wake up Friday morning, I find myself gloomy anyway. The day feels like a series of lasts. Last internship outfit, for example. Today, I'm wearing something I designed for my first *Design Diva* audition. It's a white dress with a cinched waist, full skirt, and leather accents at the shoulders. Perfect for a goodbye breakfast.

I head to the office for the last time and show Ken, the security guard, my badge.

"Have a great day, Miss Montgomery. It's been a pleasure," says Ken.

Sentimental girl that I am, my eyes start to water. I rush to the elevator, feeling silly, and take it up to the seventh floor — where it all began.

I step off the elevator and look around, remembering when Laura first gave me a tour. I look at designers working on prototypes and samples and think about the pockets I made. Someone is pinning a dress to a mannequin, and I envision the dresses I made for Taylor. I close my eyes, holding all the moments in my mind. From organizing the closet, to lugging clothes to *Vogue*, to confirming interviews for Michael, to working with models — it's all been a dream come true.

The conference room is filled with interns, all eating and chatting, when I walk in. I see Laura, Stefan, and Taylor in a corner talking with a group of interns and head to the food table to grab something to eat. I pile a bagel, eggs, fruit, and bacon onto my plate and grab a juice with my other hand, carefully carrying the items to the conference table.

"That takes some serious skill," Laura says, sliding into the seat next to me. "I was just thinking about our first meeting and my coffee-stained shirt."

I laugh. "I forgot about that. Your shirt — not the meeting."

"It feels like it was yesterday," Laura says. "I'm really going to miss having you here."

"Me too. You've taught me so much. Not only about fashion but also about how to act in this business. I'll never forget your support."

Now Laura looks choked up. She gives me a hug. "Chloe, it's been such a pleasure working with someone who's not only talented but works so hard. I know you want to be noticed. When your time comes, I'll be right there cheering you on."

"Talking to our Diva Girl?" says Stefan.

I look up, surprised. When Madison called me that, it sounded like the world's worst insult. When Stefan says it, it sounds like a compliment.

"Yes, sir," says Laura. "Just telling Chloe how much we'll miss her."

"Laura's right. You've shown a lot of promise," says Stefan. "I'd love to have you back next summer."

"I'm here if you'll have me!" I exclaim, almost knocking over my juice in excitement.

"We'd better step back when we give her the gift," Taylor says, coming up behind me. "She might jump out of her seat and spill her food on us."

I blush, but I know Taylor is just teasing. "I don't need a gift," I say. "My time here has been enough."

"Please," says Laura, waving away my words. "Ah, there's Michael. He has it."

I turn my head quickly. My time here *has* been the best gift ever, but I'd be lying if I said I wasn't intrigued by Michael's gift bag.

"Here she is," he says, handing me a black bag stuffed with silver paper. "Hope you like it."

I look around to see the other interns holding gift bags too and looking at the contents. I push the paper aside and see a Stefan Meyers gift card tucked inside.

"Oh wow!" I exclaim. "This is awesome!"

"I like my interns showing off my looks. I need all the exposure I can get," says Stefan, winking. "Buy yourself some chic back-to-school wear."

This takes back-to-school shopping to a whole new level! I picture myself in some of my favorite Stefan Meyers styles. A white sweater dress spruced up with bangle bracelets and layered with necklaces. Or maybe I'll start the year in a black ruffled skirt, knit top, and printed scarf. For a cooler day, I might go for a gray knitted pendulum sweater with stylish black boots. This gift card opens up so many possibilities!

"I think we've lost her," says Laura.

I blush. I got so caught up in my new-outfit fantasy, I forget to say thank you. "Oh my gosh, thanks so much. This is way too generous."

"There's more," says Taylor.

I look inside and gasp. It's the frayed pair of jeans I saw my first day in the closet, but that's not what makes me gasp — it's the back pockets. They're the pockets I helped design. And on the back of the pockets, where the Stefan Meyers logo normally is, someone stitched a circle with my initials intertwined — my very own CM logo.

"Remember when I told you one day you'll have your own intern and stores filled with the CM label?" asks Laura.

I nod. That was way back at the end of my second week.

"This is a start," says Laura, grinning.

"You guys, this is just amazing. I have no words," I say.

"We wanted to do something special for you," Taylor says. "Your very first CM original."

I hug the jeans to me. This is better than my name in lights.

* * *

When the breakfast is done, I finish saying my goodbyes and head back to my dorm room, walking slowly and taking in my last full day in the city.

I think about how much has changed in the past three months. What was I looking for when I auditioned for *Design Diva*? I imagined fame. I hoped for my designs to become well known. Then I won the internship, and it was as if my dreams were coming true. But I realized it was about more than recognition.

This has been such a journey. I thought I knew how everything worked, and now I know there's still so much more to learn. Even if I get to be as successful as Stefan, there's more to learn.

I take a subway to Bryant Park. I remember how the subway used to scare me. It seemed so confusing at first with all the routes laid out in different colors. Now hopping on the train feels like second nature.

At the park, I walk past the tables where Alex and I played Jenga. I think about what she said before she left: "I'm still a Santa Cruz girl at heart."

I used to think I was too. Now I'm not so sure. I listen to the honking horns and fire sirens outside the park. I look at the crowds of people and vendors. Each area of sidewalk is covered with people or stands. I find an empty bench and take out my sketchpad.

Today, I don't focus on just one person. I try to capture as many looks as I can. I draw a girl in cropped pants and a lace-up oxford with large gold hoops in her ears. I shade in the checkered pattern of another woman's minidress, then focus on her beige, wedge sandals laced up the calf. A teenaged boy in jeans and a polo shirt throws a Frisbee to his friend. I notice the Stefan Meyers logo on the boy's jeans and think of the gift Laura, Taylor, Michael, and Stefan made me. Someday people in this park will be wearing jeans with the CM logo.

I go back to the sketches I just drew and add the CM logo to the pieces. This year will be all about adding to my CM brand. That, and learning how to make my designs crisper. And when I see Stefan again next summer, he'll see how far this California girl has come.

CM

CM

Soon at a BOUTIQUE NEAR YOU!

♡ a JUMPSUIT!

✓ BLACK and WHITE CHECK

Beige WEDGE BOOTS

Author Bio

Margaret Gurevich has wanted to be a
writer since second grade and has written
for many magazines, including *Girls' Life*,
SELF, and *Ladies' Home Journal*. Her first
young adult novel, *Inconvenient*, was a Sydney
Taylor Notable Book for Teens, and her second novel,
Pieces of Us, garnered positive reviews from *Kirkus*, *VOYA*, and
Publishers Weekly, which called it "painfully believable." When not
writing, Margaret enjoys hiking, cooking, reading, watching too
much television, and spending time with her husband and son.

MARGIE

Illustrator Bio

Brooke Hagel is a fashion illustrator
based in New York City. While studying
fashion design at the Fashion Institute
of Technology, she began her career
as an intern, working in the wardrobe
department of *Sex and the City*, the design
studios of Cynthia Rowley, and the production
offices of *Saturday Night Live*. After graduating, Brooke began
designing and styling for Hearst Magazines, contributing to *Harper's
Bazaar*, *House Beautiful*, *Seventeen*, and *Esquire*. Brooke is now a
successful illustrator with clients including *Vogue*, *Teen Vogue*, *InStyle*,
Dior, Brian Atwood, Hugo Boss, Barbie, Gap, and Neutrogena.

BROOKE